Once, in a place at the bottom of the ocean that is deeper, darker, further, wetter, colder, lonelier than anything you can imagine, there lived a Piglet Squid.

Soon, he met a swallower fish.

"Do you know what there
is to smile about?"
he asked the swallower fish.

more of a mystery . . .
than anything that can be imagined.

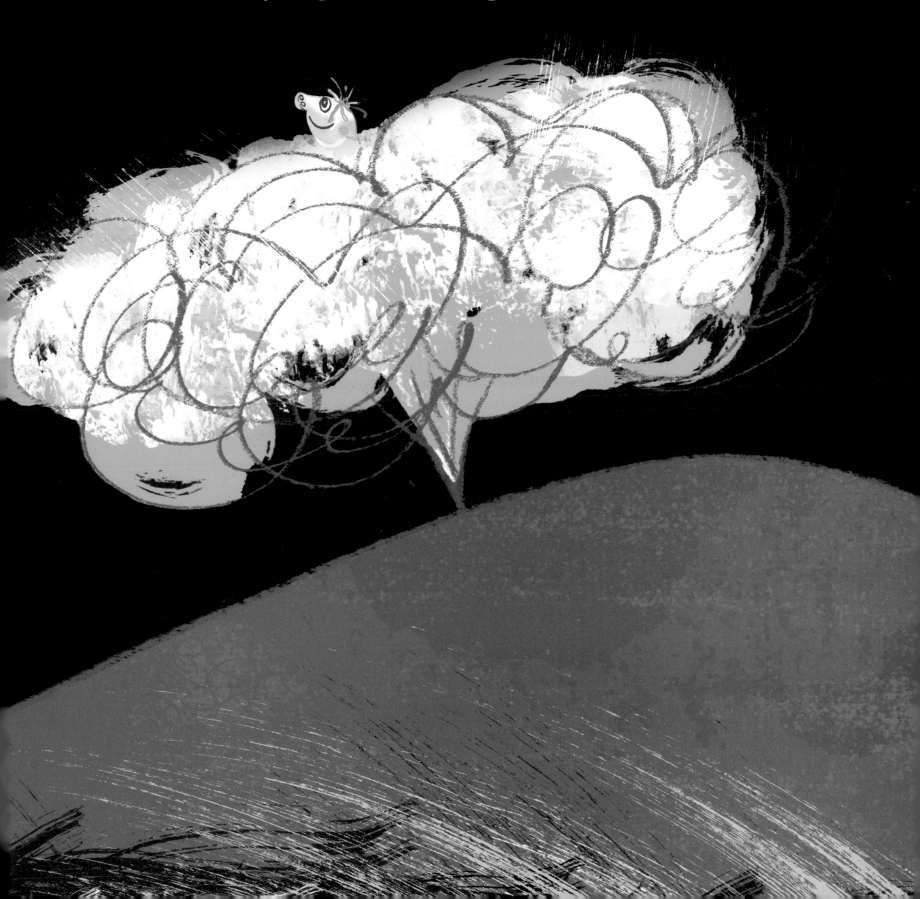

And all around the face,
endlessly shining and twinkling,
were hundreds and thousands,
and millions and billions
of shiny things,
all smiling.

Piglet Squid smiled at the face. The face smiled back. Oh, such a smile!